8

TITLE IX ROCKS!
PLAY LIKE A GIRL™

FIGURE SKATING
GIRLS ROCKING IT

PETE MICHALSKI and KATHRYN M. MONCRIEF

ROSEN
PUBLISHING

NEW YORK

Published in 2016 by The Rosen Publishing Group, Inc.
29 East 21st Street, New York, NY 10010

First Edition

Library of Congress Cataloging-in-Publication Data

Michalski, Pete.
Figure skating / by Pete Michalski and Kathryn M. Moncrief p. cm. — (Title IX
rocks)
Includes bibliographical references and index.
ISBN 978-1-5081-7033-4 (library binding)
1. Figure skating for girls—Juvenile literature. 2. Women figure skaters—
Juvenile literature. 3. Ice skating—Juvenile literature. I. Michalski, Pete II.
Moncrief, Kathryn M III. Title.
GV850.4 M64 2016
796.91'2'082—d23

Manufactured in China

CONTENTS

The sound of metal skates hitting the ice, the crisp, cold air, and the speed and grace can be infectious, almost addicting. Developing flexibility, athletic talent, and just plain having a great time are other benefits to one of the most beloved sports. Figure skating is one of the most dynamic and enjoyable individual sports out there. It is an exciting sport, and many consider it to be an art form, too, much like ballet and other forms of dance.

Ice skating has been around for many centuries, and probably developed as a true sport simultaneously in Scotland and the Netherlands. It has advanced in leaps and bounds since the 19th century to become one of the most popular individual sports, both for participants and for spectators. From the 20th century through the present day, figure skaters have been among the most idolized and admired athletes of our time. Girls and young women in particular have made the sport what is it today and put it on the map.

The name "figure skating" comes from the shapes that skaters carve in the ice, a result of their motion and skate blades working together. For a very long time, up until 1990, a big part of the sport was actually creating these figures and retracing them on the ice in order to score points with competition judges. As many as eighty figures were skated in a single competition, and points were scored

Mao Asada free skates at the World Figure Skating Championships in Japan, her homeland, on March 29, 2014. Like other champions of the sport, her rise to the top took a tremendous amount of effort.

according to how well this tracing was performed and the superior posture of the skaters. While tracing figures was eliminated in 1990, the name of the sport has remained the same. Some skaters, however, miss the figures because of the level of focus and discipline as well as the special skills, especially the emphasis on edges and control, that figures brought to the sport.

There has probably never been a better time to be a female athlete—and a female figure skater—than now. Part of the reason is that, for the last few decades, Title IX has been the law of the land. This 1972 law outlawed discrimination against girls and women in all educational programs that receive federal government funding. This has included access to higher education, math and science learning, technology, and other fields. But it is perhaps best known for pushing many institutions to provide fair amounts of funding for female athletics.

While ensuring parity with boys and men's sports programs still has a long way to go, Title IX helped female athletes tremendously, including figure skaters. Hugely popular among girls even before Title IX, figure skating arrived and never went away. The athleticism, power, and grace it requires has made it among the most demanding and time-consuming sports to compete in at the highest levels.

Modern skating is a multimillion-dollar activity with competitions, shows, and tours, and skating champions can become well-known celebrities. It is also a sport that can be enjoyed by girls and women of all ages and sizes, from two years old up to women in their seventies. Time to hit the ice and enter the thrilling world of figure skating!

CHAPTER ONE

A SPORT AND ARTFORM

Ice-skating has a long history. It began in what is now northern Europe thousands of years ago. First bone runners and then metal runners were strapped to shoes. The first skating club was formed in Edinburgh, Scotland, in 1742. But it wasn't until 1850 that figure skates with the blades permanently attached to boots were invented, and figure skating in both Europe and North America really took off. Skating clubs began holding competitions and ice carnivals.

The oldest skating club in the United States, the Philadelphia Skating Club and Humane Society, was incorporated in 1861. Compared to nowadays, figure skating then was stiff and formal. Then, in the 1860s, an American skater, Jackson Haines, revolutionized skating by incorporating dance moves and skating to music in his routines. His signature moves included a sit-spin and a spiral

This illustration from 1891 depicts a woman giving a lesson in cutting figures on the ice, the activity that gave the sport its name.

He skated on tour, and his style quickly caught on.

In 1892, what is now the International Skating Union (ISU) was formed to govern speed- and ice-skating. Now, the ISU has more than fifty member countries. There are competitive skaters from countries as diverse as the United States, Canada, China, Russia, Uzbekistan, and Thailand.

At first, competitive figure skating was considered a man's sport. People believed it was unsuitable for a woman to pursue such an athletic activity or to show her legs when her skirt came up a bit during jumps. In 1902, Madge Syers of Great Britain shocked the skating world by entering and coming in second in the men's world championships. In 1903, women were officially barred! But women weren't about to give up. In 1906, a separate ladies' event was introduced. Madge Syers went on to win the ladies' world gold medal in both 1906 and 1907, as well as the 1908 Olympic gold medal, when skating first appeared at the summer games. In 1924, when the separate winter Olympics were first started, skating became, as it is today, a part of the winter games.

In the 1920s and 1930s, another famous skater, Sonja Henie of Norway, captured the public's imagination and had a major impact on the popularity of the sport. She was only eleven years old when she competed in her first Olympics in 1924. She came in eighth. However, by 1927, at age fourteen, she was the world champion. Altogether, she won ten world titles and three Olympic gold medals. After she retired from amateur competition, she toured in popular ice shows and even became a film star. Henie was especially

Sonja Henie of Norway, one of skating's legends, competes at her first Olympics. She was only eleven at the time, beginning a winning career that would make her an international star.

known for her dazzling skating skills, which combined ballet with skating, and for her innovative, glamorous costumes. Before Henie, women skated in long skirts for the sake of modesty. Because she was so young, she was able to wear short dresses, then considered too provocative for older girls, and thus was able to do spins and jumps that had been impossible in more cumbersome clothing. Also, Henie was the first to make famous the white figure skating boots that are common for women figure skaters today.

In the 1940s and 1950s, in the wake of Henie's prosperous film career, ice rinks were built all over the United States. The 1956 and 1960 Olympic ladies champions, Tenley Albright and Carol Heiss, were both from the United States.

Then, in 1961, there was a terrible tragedy. A plane carrying the entire U.S. figure skating team, bound for the world championships in Prague, crashed. Everyone on board the plane—all the skaters, their coaches, and many of their family members—were killed. In the aftermath, skating programs in the United States had to rebuild. Many top European coaches went to the United States. This included Carlo Fassi, who would coach Peggy Fleming and Dorothy Hamill to their Olympic gold medals. Today, the U.S. Figure Skating Association has a memorial fund in the names of the victims of the crash to help skaters with training costs.

In 1994, associates of skater Tonya Harding attacked her rival, Nancy Kerrigan, after a practice session at the U.S. national championships in Detroit. Televised images of the stunned Kerrigan clutching her knee riveted viewers, and the weeks leading to the 1994 Olympic Games became a soap opera. Ironically, and perhaps sadly for those involved, skating benefited from the exposure as interest in the sport reached unprecedented levels. The short program in the Olympic Games, where Nancy Kerrigan and Tonya Harding met each other in competition, remains one of the most-watched television programs of

Tonya Harding is shown here practicing at the 1994 Olympics, with her rival Nancy Kerrigan in the background. Their rivalry would inadvertently popularize skating again.

all time. Sixteen-year-old Oksana Baiul, an orphan from the Ukraine, captured the gold medal in the midst of all the scandal.

HITTING THE RINK

There are ice rinks located in almost every town and city. Check your local mall, school, recreation center, or specialized skating facility for ice times. You will find "public sessions," which are times that allow all skaters on the ice. Public sessions are inexpensive, but they can be a nuisance for anyone who is there to practice figure skating skills. The rink can be crowded with skaters of all ability levels. Skating is limited to one direction with only the center reserved for figure skating practice.

THE POPULARITY OF MODERN FIGURE SKATING

While figure skating still enjoys wide popularity as an activity around the United States and Canada, as of the 2010s, its status as a cultural phenomenon and spectator sport in the United States has seen better days. There has been somewhat of a decline in television ratings as well as in live, in-person attendance rates since the 1990s and early 2000s. Major tours that used to feature big stars of figure skating have declined or folded. Part of this may have been the greater success of other female sports, such as soccer and, perhaps surprisingly, snowboarding. The *Wall Street Journal* reported in February 2014 that the USFSA reported that annual membership has remained steady and healthy.

Other observers believe that possibly confusing changes in the way that judges score competitions, along with other changes in regulation, have made the sport less appealing to fans. Audiences may also be waiting for a new crop of recognizable stars, especially in singles competition. On the other hand, other nations have seen a rise in figure skating's popularity, including near pop-star-like status for South Korea's Yuna Kim (the 2014 Olympic Silver medalist) and Japan's Mao Asada in their home countries. Whatever the case, diehard skating fans think that the lull in popularity is cyclical, and that

figure skating will once again bounce back in the coming years.

Instead, you may want to look for "freestyle sessions," which give freestyle skaters a chance to practice. These are often divided into high and low levels of ability. Although they're more expensive than public sessions, the ice is reserved expressly for figure skaters. Other sessions may be reserved specifically for ice dancing. Some rinks host special "for adults only" or family nights. Pick a session that suits your ability level and skating preference.

Finally, the rink may offer a special time available only to members of the local figure skating club. Consider becoming a member of the club. There will be a fee to join, but benefits include reserved ice sessions, socializing, and other member privileges.

GEARING UP

You won't need to make a big investment to get started in figure skating, but at the very minimum you will need a pair of skates and some workout clothes.

How to Pick Skates

Skates consist of boots and blades. Try rental skates first, and when you're sure you want to continue, invest in your own pair. If you do continue to skate, you will soon want to have your own skates. To keep costs down, look for a used, but not broken down, pair of boots to begin. Do not buy boots with deep crevices and signs of excessive wear. Try your local pro shop, or check bulletin

Kaitlyn Weaver laces up before the ISU World Championships in 2012 at Budweiser Gardens in London, Ontario. The right skates are your first step to skating excellence.

boards at your rink for leads on good-quality used skates.

Whether you are skating in rental skates or your own pair, find skates that fit and feel good on your feet. Properly fitted boots and blades will increase your comfort and will help your skating. Boots should be snug but not tight, and your foot should not move in the heel. Instead of heavy socks or double layers of socks, wear tights or light stockings. Lace your skates so they are snug at the toes but a little looser around your ankles so they can move when you bend your knees. Ask a coach or a professional at your local pro shop to help you find the best fit. Look for leather soles, not molded plastic ones, and steel blades that can be sharpened. Avoid inexpensive hardware or discount store skates. Reputable brands include Jackson, GAM, Risport, Reidell, and SP-Teri.

Be careful not to purchase "too much boot." Boots that are too advanced, or too thick and heavy for your skating level will be more difficult for you to break in and will hinder your progress. Boots need the right amount of padding and stiffness to support you when you skate. As you progress (in other words, as you jump more), you will need thicker boots to withstand the additional pressure.

Boots can be very uncomfortable at first and can take time to break in. Be patient about finding the right pair and getting a good fit. The boots, along with your blades, are your most important pieces of equipment. As you advance as a skater, you may eventually want to consider custom boots made just for you. These are more expensive, but they'll be precisely constructed both for your feet and for the type of training you do.

As a beginner, you can purchase stock (premade) boots with blades already mounted. A beginning boot and blade combination costs approximately $100 to $240. When you purchase higher-quality skates, boots and blades will be sold separately.

As with choosing your boots, you must select blades that are appropriate for your size, ability, and the type of skating you do. For example, ice-dance blades are shorter and have smaller toe picks than do freestyle blades. This is because ice dancers do not execute jumps like freestyle skaters, who need large picks to help them vault into the air. Blades differ in radius (how curved they are), hollowness (the groove between the edges), and toe pick. Again, work with your coach or a pro in selecting blades. Blades will cost between $200 and $600. A professional will sharpen and mount your blades to your boots.

How long your skates will last depends on how often you train (especially how much you jump) and how much you grow. If you train on an elite level, your skates will last for about six months to a year, and your blades for about nine months. If you are a recreational skater, they will last much longer. You can use your boots until they are broken down (until they no longer provide you with proper support) and your blades until they can no longer be sharpened.

Blades should always be kept sharp and in good condition. New blades need to be sharpened before you first use them. After that, they'll need sharpening about once a month, depending on how much skating you do. Have a professional sharpen your blades.

Skate Guards

Skate guards, which are rubber covers for your blades, protect them from nicks, pebbles, and dirt on the floor after you put on your boots. Never walk with your skates on without your guards, even for short distances. Remember to remove the guards before you step out onto the ice. Everyone has made that mistake at least once. The hard fall that results should be enough to remind you to take the guards off the next time. You will also need a pair of soakers (terry cloth blade covers) to protect your blades from moisture.

After you skate, be sure to wipe your blades dry with a towel to prevent rust and to cover the blades with your soakers. Remember not to store your skates in a closed bag when you get home. Remove them so they can air out and dry. Periodically, you will want to polish your boots (especially before a test or a competition) to keep them looking fresh.

Clothing to Practice In

Clothing for practice should be warm and comfortable, and it should allow you to move. Street clothes, such as jeans, will not give you the necessary flexibility, but you don't need special costumes or expensive dance clothes for practice either. Workout clothes, a simple skating dress, a leotard and tights, or leggings and a T-shirt are perfectly acceptable. Cover up with a sweater, sweatshirt, or warm-up jacket and sweatpants or leg warmers you can take off

Dressing for the environment, whether outside or indoors, means dressing warmly. But your clothing should be flexible enough so you can move around comfortably.

when you get hot. You should have a pair of light, stretchy gloves to keep your hands warm and to protect them when you fall. You might also want a pair of boot covers if you find that your toes get too cold. Finally, if you have long hair, you will want to wear it in a ponytail or braid to keep your hair out of your face.

Protecting Yourself

Many beginners use pads and helmets to help prevent injury. A good bicycle helmet will do. You may also want wrist guards like those used for in-line skating, as well as soft elbow and knee-pads. These items are readily available at any sporting goods store.

Miscellaneous Items

There are other miscellaneous items that will make skating more pleasant and comfortable. Many people find that the cold air of a rink (or the outdoors) makes their noses run. Stock up on tissues and bring them with you to practice. Gel pads, such as the brand-name Bunga Pads, are good to slip into your skates to keep irritation from rubbing to a minimum. You can also use foam pads, including makeup sponges. Athletic tape or bandages under your boots help prevent (and treat) blisters, too. You should also keep spare laces on you, as well extra gloves, tights, and socks, just in case. To prevent chapped lips from the cold or dryness, bring lip balm.

CHAPTER TWO

SKILLS AND CONFIDENCE ON THE ICE

Entering the higher echelons of professional skating takes years of training and dedication. Before you can waltz jump, you need to be able to execute a bunny hop. From there, you need to master the other single-rotation jumps, and then move on to axel jumps. The skills needed for skating are complex and cumulative— the more advanced ones are built on the foundations of the more basic ones before them. Single jumps come before doubles and triples, for example.

It's like learning to play a musical instrument: You must first learn the basic skills, then practice them until they are part of you. Some jumps and spins take years to perfect. But you can gain a sense of accomplishment as you learn and become proficient at each new skill on the way to achieving your goals in the sport. Talent and nat- ural physical ability certainly help, but excellence in figure skating also takes mental and emotional fortitude. Skating requires desire, focus, dedication, and practice. Most of all, it should be something you enjoy doing. You don't have to begin skating at age three or be a size three to skate either. Skating is a sport that anyone can enjoy.

STARTING OUT

The best way to get started is to join a "learn to skate" program at your local rink. The Ice Skating Institute (ISI), the United States Figure Skating Association (USFSA), and Skate Canada all have "learn to skate" programs. All three administer tests and host competitions, and all three

Many figure skaters who hope to compete start earlier rather than later. Regardless, everyone must learn the basics and be patient and persistent.

have very good, structured programs for learning basic skating skills. The ISI focuses its attention primarily on the recreational skater. The USFSA and Skate Canada, as the national governing bodies for skating in the United States and Canada, are more oriented toward the competitive (Olympic-eligible) skater. Being a member of one of these organizations also makes you eligible to participate in their testing and competition system.

A series of group lessons will cover basic skills, including proper stroking, gliding, falling, and stopping. It will then progress to turns, beginning spins, and jumps. You can learn all of your basic skills and beginning freestyle moves in a group lesson program. Group lessons will cost about $80 for eight one-hour, weekly lessons. Each session will include both instruction and practice time.

GETTING A COACH

If you continue in skating, and if you want to test and compete, you will want to hire a coach to work one-on-one with you in private lessons. With a private coach, you will learn more skills more quickly, and you will have more attention and supervision, as well as help in developing a competitive program. Coaching varies in cost, but it usually ranges from $35 to $100 per hour, depending on the area of the country and the level of experience or fame a coach has.

Finding a good coach, like finding the right boots, is about fit. Check the coach's professional credentials. Your rink should have information about professional coaches who teach there. With whom did he or she train? What was his or her competitive record? Which tests has the coach passed? Is the coach a member of the Professional Skaters Association (PSA)? What kind of skating and teaching experience does he or she have? What kind of professional experience does he or she have?

It isn't necessary for your coach to have been an Olympic medalist to be an excellent teacher. The reverse is true as well; winning a gold medal does not guarantee that he or she is a good teacher. Ask other skaters about their coaches and observe the coaches with their students while you are choosing. Are the students happy with their coaches? Does the coach treat his or her students with respect? Are the students achieving their goals in skating, and are they satisfied with their progress?

Your coach should be someone who can communicate skating skills and principles to you. He or she should be positive and should

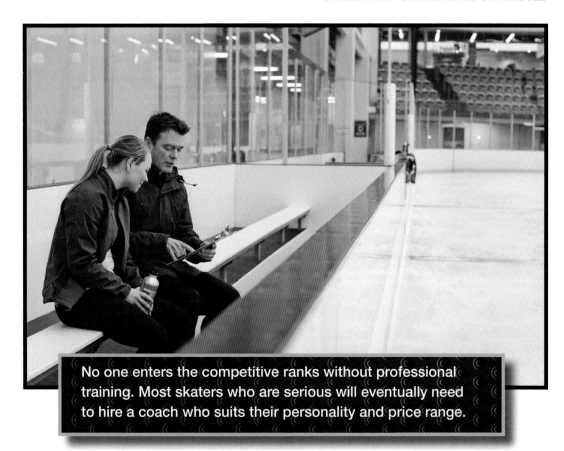

No one enters the competitive ranks without professional training. Most skaters who are serious will eventually need to hire a coach who suits their personality and price range.

have your safety and well-being, as well as your long-term goals and interests, in mind. A good coach will prepare you mentally and physically to set and achieve your goals in skating. You should feel comfortable with your coach, as this is someone with whom you will spend a great deal of time.

The amount of time you spend training will vary, depending on your skating goals. You may be content taking a lesson once or twice a week and practicing your skating in public sessions. However, if you plan to compete, you will need a more demanding practice schedule. Top skaters need six or more on-ice sessions each day, plus daily lessons, in addition to off-ice training (dance and conditioning). Many high-level skaters also hire special-ists—such as a spin coach, a specialized choreographer, a ballet instructor, or a sports psychologist—to work with them in addition to their primary coach.

Remember to make the most of your coaching and practice time. Both are expensive. You will want to prepare in advance for your lessons and practice your skills on your own. You will also want to be attentive and willing to work with your coach during your lesson. Your willingness to learn and your work ethic are necessary parts of achieving your skating goals.

SKATING BLADES 101

One of the most important things to know about figure skating is that skating blades are not flat; they have edges. Each skate has an inside edge, corresponding with the inside of the leg, and an outside edge. The middle of the blade has a slight hollow. Most skating moves take place on edges, not on the middle (the "flat") part of the skate. Also, each skate can move forward and backward. Altogether, there are eight directions: forward right inside, forward right outside, forward left inside, forward left outside, back right inside, back right outside, back left inside, and back left outside. Many moves you will learn, such as the "three-turn" (so called because it traces a pattern like the number three in the ice), can be done in each direction. For example, one can skate a forward right three-turn starting on a forward outside edge and then turning around to end up on a backward inside edge.

STEPPING OUT ON THE ICE

Once you have your skates laced, you are ready to begin skating. Remember to remove your skate guards before you step onto the ice. Bend your knees slightly and balance your weight over your

Achieving good, basic form comes before trying anything too showy. The first few times on the ice might be difficult and tiring, but it will eventually get easier the more often you practice.

skates. Do not lean forward, but keep your shoulders over your hips. Hold your arms out, slightly in front of you, between waist- and chest-level. Look up at where you are going, not down at your feet. Now, take a couple of small marching steps, then let yourself glide a little on both feet. Repeat this several times. Don't forget to rest when you feel tired. You are asking your muscles to behave in unfamiliar ways, so don't overdo it at first. Some of the first things you will learn in group lessons will be the following:

Skating Forward (Stroking)

With your knees bent, you will push off from the middle of one blade, then will glide on the opposite blade and will continue,

KINDS OF JUMPS (FROM LEAST TO MOST DIFFICULT)

Waltz jump A basic half jump, the foundation of the axel. It begins going forward on a left outside edge and lands on the right outside edge of the opposite foot.

Toe loop A toe jump that takes off from a back outside edge, assisted by pushing up and off the opposite toe pick, and lands on the same back outside edge. The same jump is a toe walley when taking off from the inside edge.

Salchow An edge jump that takes off from the back inside edge and lands on the back outside edge of the opposite foot. It was invented by Ulrich Salchow of Sweden.

Loop Jump An edge jump that takes off and lands from the back outside edge of the same foot. This jump is sometimes called a Rittberger after Germany's Werner Rittberger, the person who first invented it.

Flip jump A toe jump that takes off from the back inside edge, assisted by the toe pick, and lands on the back outside edge of the opposite foot.

Lutz jump A toe jump invented by Austrian skater Alois Lutz that takes off from a long, back outside edge, assisted by the toe pick, and lands on the back outside edge of the opposite foot. An intended lutz that switches to an inside edge is often referred to as a "flutz."

Axel jump An edge jump that takes off from a forward outside edge and lands on the back outside edge of the opposite foot. This is considered the most difficult jump because it rotates an extra half turn in the air. For example, a triple axel rotates three and one half times. It was invented by Norway's Axel Paulsen.

A figure skater in mid-air is about to land a triple axel, one of figure skating's most difficult maneuvers.

alternating your weight from one blade to the other. Place your feet in a T position, left foot straight ahead of you, the right foot perpendicular behind you with the heel of your left skate at the arch of the right foot. (Your feet will form the T.) Push off with the right foot and allow yourself to glide forward on the left. Keep your free leg off the ice and extended behind you with your leg turned out as you push, then bring it back to you and shift your weight onto it. Push off with the opposite leg. Repeat and continue.

Snowplow Stop

Once you learn to go forward, you will need to know how to stop. The snowplow stop is the easiest way to stop your forward momentum. Point the toes of your skate together to make an upside-down V shape, like the front a snowplow. Press down and out with the inside of both blades, remembering to keep your knees bent, until you come to a stop. Skate blades move smoothly across the ice only in a forward or backward motion. Here, you are scraping the blade in a sideways motion, which will bring you to a stop. You can also do this stop by turning in just one foot, instead of both feet. In this case, continue gliding on one foot, but turn in the toe of the other blade. Press down and out until you come to a stop.

Two-Foot Turn

Gliding forward on two feet, rotate your upper body in a clockwise or counterclockwise direction. Let your hip follow, letting your body work like a spring as you turn from going forward to backward.

Off-Ice Training

In addition to lessons and practice at the rink, you can also partici- pate in other activities to enhance your skating. These include weight training and dance classes, including jazz, modern, ballet, or oth- ers. Consult with your coach to determine which activities are best for you.

Nutrition

One potential pitfall of trying to excel in sports is having unre- alistic expectations when it comes to your physique. Like other activities—such as bal- let, for example—figure skating is a performance sport. Many girls feel the pressure to conform to a particular body ideal, both to look better while performing, and to be able to execute

Ballet can provide the rigorous workout and help develop the poise, grace, and stamina that is required for figure skating.

some of the more demanding skating routines, and look good doing it. It is very important not to starve oneself or fast to try and quickly get down to a certain weight or size. It not only drains you of the necessary energy for your training and performances, it can be extremely dangerous. A balanced and healthy diet will go much further in helping you excel and develop the kind of body that is right for you to perform your best. If you are concerned about your body, consult a physician, and they will confirm that this is indeed the best advice. They will also warn you that doing fad diets or taking any kind of weight-loss drugs are unhealthy and dangerous ideas, too.

CHAPTER THREE

RULES AND ADVICE

F igure skaters with aspirations to rise to the top of their sport have a clear path ahead of them. Local competitions feed into regional contests. A figure skater then graduates onto the national competition scene. The end goal is becoming a national champion and hopefully scoring a world championship, the most prestigious of which is an Olympic gold medal. However, training, testing, and competition mean more than just medals,. It is perhaps most important that you challenge yourself and satisfy your own goals. Winning medals and championships can motivate you to do so, but competing or not is a personal choice. It is perfectly okay to enjoy skating—merely to improve yourself—without ever testing or competing.

Even young children can get good enough at an early age to train at a competitive level. These two siblings are skating at the Nathan Phillips Square skating rink in Toronto, Ontario.

TESTS: CLIMBING THE RANKS

Once you learn to skate, you should take tests administered by the USFSA, the ISI, or Skate Canada. You can test just for the personal satisfaction of knowing what you have accomplished. But if you choose to compete, you will need to test to determine your level of competition. The skaters you see on television are, with only a few exceptions, senior or championship-level skaters. However, there are many competitive levels below the senior level and most skaters are in the lower levels, working their way up. The USFSA levels, beginning at the bottom, are pre-preliminary, preliminary, prejuvenile, juvenile, intermediate, novice, junior, and senior.

In the ISI system, staff members administer tests. You can earn badges when you compete at each level. ISI levels, from the lowest to the highest, are pre-alpha, alpha, beta, gamma, and delta. Once you have passed the delta test, you can begin working on freestyle levels, beginning at freestyle 1. You can test at each level anytime you and your coach decide you are ready. Information on ISI testing is available by contacting the ISI, including consulting their website.

The USFSA is more regimented because it is oriented toward competitive skaters. Coaches administer tests only at the lowest levels. Test sessions must by sanctioned by the USFSA board of directors and are judged by qualified officials. The panel of judges (usually three) watches your performance and gives you a "pass" or a "retry," meaning you will have to take the test again in the future to advance. The judges may also supply comments for

Judges watch the ice at the 2005 U.S. Figure Skating Championships at the Rose Garden in Portland, Oregon. Judges are under scrutiny now because of scandals in the early 2000s.

your improvement. Contact the USFSA for information on testing requirements and procedures.

COMPETING

Whatever your skating goals, there are many types of competitions at every level of ability, from local and club events to national and international events. Whether you plan to compete in the nationals or an interclub competition, competitions can be both motivating and fun.

ISI

The ISI, focusing on the recreational skater, offers many different competitions, including events for solo dancers, small children,

A team of young women from a figure skating school performs in Barcelona, Spain, in May 2014. Schools and school programs are another way to learn and develop one's skills.

skaters with disabilities, comedy teams, production numbers, interpretive skaters, and so on.

USFSA

The USFSA, geared more toward Olympic-eligible competitors, offers both invitational events (stand-alone competitions hosted by skating clubs) and qualifying events (those that determine eligibility for higher-level competitions and national or Olympic teams). The rules for USFSA competitions are specified by the International Skating Union (ISU), which is the governing body for figure skating. An ISU committee meets regularly to review and to revise rules. Be certain that you and your coach are aware of the most recent rule changes when you are preparing for competition.

A system of qualifying events on the regional, sectional, and national levels begins in the fall and culminates in the junior nationals for juvenile and intermediate skaters, and the senior nationals for novice, junior, and senior skaters. Regional and sectional competitions determine who will qualify for nationals. Only four skaters from each section—Pacific coast, Midwestern and Eastern—advance to nationals. Other skaters, including champions from the previous year, are also allowed to compete. The national championships determine who will represent the country on world and Olympic teams, though a selection committee has the final say. Also in the fall, junior and senior international competitions that lead to a grand prix final take place, as do the European and the Four Continents championships. The final and most prestigious event in non-Olympic years is the world championship. The number of competitors that each country is allowed is determined by that country's placing in the previous year's world championship, but each country may send only three skaters at most.

American Gracie Gold takes a jubilant leap during the gala exhibition at the 2005 World Team Trophy Figure Skating Championships in Tokyo, Japan.

Scoring

A skating competition is scored by a panel of judges. In 2004, a longstanding point system (in which 6.0 was the highest, and perfect, score) was replaced with an entirely new one. This was done in response to a score-fixing scandal among Olympic judges in 2002. In the new system, all points are cumulative, and there is no perfect score. Skaters receive a base point value for each move they perform in a program. This point value is based on difficulty. They get this basic score for the attempt, and not the successful execution. That is why, while it does not happen often, a skater can fall and still score higher than a competitor who skated a clean program.

Beyond these base point values, judges can give or subtract up to three points from each move. A fall means a mandatory deduction of one point from that maneuver. There are five elements the skaters are also scored on: choreography, skating skill, transition, execution, and interpretation. These are scores given for a whole program, and each of these can be scored from one-fourth of a point, to a total of 10 points. A technical specialist tracks and confirms the elements performed and completed, which determines a total base value. The judges then add their grades for execution of the technical elements, and their scores for the five program components.

The final score is partially determined via computer, which randomly selects the scores of seven out of the nine total judges. Of these seven, the lowest and highest scores are thrown out, and the five remaining scores are totaled for the final score. All nine judges' marks are displayed publicly at the competition. Thus, it is almost impossible to figure out which judges' determinations went into the final scoring. This system was set up to prevent judges rigging competitions, after some scandal and controversy erupted in the 2002 Salt Lake City Olympics, when two judges, from France and Russia respectively, were discovered colluding to help each other's nation's competitors. In the new system, winning scores are about 200 or a bit higher for women's figure skating.

Short Program and Long Program (Free Skate)

The junior- or senior-level short program lasts for up to two minutes and fifty seconds. It is made up of eight element requirements, taken from among the various jumps, spins, and footwork sequences allowed. Missed or failed elements result in

Zahra Lari of the United Arab Emirates (UAE) practices at a rink in Abu Dhabi, her nation's capital, aiming to be an Emirati competitor in Olympic figure skating.

a mandatory deduction from the judges' scorecards. The short program accounts for one-third of a skater's total score in competition.

The other two-thirds of a competition score is made of the junior or senior free skate. Also called free skating or the long program, it usually follows the short program and lasts four minutes, plus or minus 10 seconds. Before 2004, the free skate had no specific requirements. A skater would perform whatever combination of moves that best demonstrated her particular skills and strengths. After the new judging system was implemented, the free skate ceased to really be free, and simply became the long program. Now a skater must make seven jumping passes, three spins, a step sequence, and a choreographic sequences (although junior free skates omit this last requirement). Some applaud the new system for making it more transparent to score technical prowess, while others believe some of the artistry and grace has been compromised.

INVESTING IN SKATING

Those who have potential and talent—and the drive and desire to realize them—need to consider the costs involved with pursuing their dreams of figure skating competitively. For every year they skate, they can expect to fork over at least $10,000 and up to $20,000 to retain a good coach. Ice time can cost in the thousands, while costumes, clothing, and new sets of boots and blades can range between $4,000 and $6,000. Other expenses include thousands of dollars of travel to get to skating competitions. Entry fees for competitions can cost at least $1,000 annually.

Skating on a high level at a top training facility can be prohibitively costly. Many parents take second jobs, mortgage their homes, and make crosscountry moves to better support their child's skating ambitions. However, skating at a city recreational facility or a mall rink, many of which have good ice surfaces and qualified coaches, can be a lot cheaper—and a lot of fun.

A truly thrifty family or skater can perhaps get away with spending as little as $20,000, but often the costs can exceed that. It depends entirely on how much time and effort one is willing to put in, as well as how much disposable cash they have on hand. However, anyone with serious ambitions of excelling in the sport should naturally expect to pay more, not less.

French figure skater Maé-Bérénice Méité does a graceful haircutter spin in Bordeaux, France. Her costume is a good example of the kind most high-level competitors skate in.

COSTUMES AND CHOREOGRAPHY

For some test sessions and for competition, you will need special costumes, music, and choreography. If you choose to compete, you need to work with a coach to create your programs. High-level and elite skaters may also work with choreographers, in addition to their coaches, to create programs. Many skaters often work only with a coach as they develop their programs and select their music. Costumes can be simple or very elaborate, but they should fit you well and should not restrict your movement. They should suit your body type, coloring, program, and the type of skating

Music inspires the crowd, the judges, and the skater herself. China's Li Zijun takes flight during a free skate program in 2013 with the music from *Sleeping Beauty* as her soundtrack.

you do (balletic, jazzy, etc.). Don't wear a frilly peasant dress if it doesn't make sense with the music or if you are uncomfortable in it. Your costume will be part of your presentation and will enhance your program.

Over the years, costumes have become more important and more costly. In 1976, Dorothy Hamill skated in the Olympics in a $75 costume her mother had made for her. By contrast, in the 1994 Olympics, Nancy Kerrigan's free-skating costume, worth $13,000, featured 11,500 rhinestones and was made by top fashion designer (and former figure skater) Vera Wang.

These days, an average skating costume worn by championship-level figure skaters, according to a 2014 broadcast of National Pulic Radio's *Marketplace* program, can run between $1,500 and $5,000. Gracie Gold's February 2014 *Sports Illustrated* cover showed the figure skater in a $3,000 dress.

But don't worry, your costume does not have to cost a small fortune to be beautiful and appropriate. A pretty leotard and wrap-around skirt with a few added details (such as ribbons or spangles) can make a terrific costume.

As with your costume, music and choreography should be matched to your style and ability, should highlight your strengths, and should help you show your skating at its best. Your coach will work with you to choose and edit suitable music and to develop choreography to show off your best skills. You will want to choose music that both suits your personal style and fits the requirements for the competition.

ELIGIBLE VERSUS INELIGIBLE

Skaters used to be divided into amateur and professional ranks. Amateurs weren't allowed to make any money from skating.

Now, skaters are considered either "eligible," meaning they are allowed, according to International Skating Union rules, to compete in Olympic competitions, or "ineligible," meaning they may not do so. Many professional-only competitions are not sanctioned by the ISU, so a skater could lose her Olympic eligibility by skating in one. However, there are many competitions and tours open to eligible skaters and pros alike. Be careful to enter only sanctioned competitions and events.

CHAPTER FOUR

GOING FOR IT: BEING A PRO

I f they start in their early teen years, young women who choose to skate in competition can look forward to about a decade and a half of professional competition ahead of them. ABC News reported in 2014 that the average female figure skater was about 22.27 years old. Maria Butyrskaya of Russia, the 1999 world champion, was twenty-six years old when she won her world gold medal, and she was one of the oldest to win international titles at age 29. She was the oldest to win international medals.

Realistically, very few skaters ever make it to championship-level skating and to the Olympic Games. A maximum of three female skaters from each country is allowed to compete in the Olympics, and only one gold medal is awarded every four years. On top of that, the chances of becoming an Olympic gold medalist are very slim. If you are investing in skating only to win a gold medal, you may be disappointed. Ask yourself why you want to skate. What do you hope to achieve? How much time and money are you able to devote to it?

Though the odds are against winning an individual Olympic or world medal, there are several other paths to take in competitive or professional skating. You may want to try pair skating, ice dancing, or synchronized skating. Many skaters get jobs in touring ice shows such as *Broadway on Ice* or *Disney on Ice.* These shows employ not only former Olympians, but also supporting skaters and extras. Others find that their talents lie in teaching and work as coaches or choreographers. Some former skaters even work as sports journalists. Then again, many girls and women skate recreationally all of their lives, are happy with the sport as they perform it, and are satisfied never to compete.

MODERN STARS OF SKATING

One of the biggest modern stars of skating retired some years back. Michelle Kwan, 1998 Olympic silver medalist, was born in Torrence, California, on July 7, 1980. She began skating when she was five years old after watching her older brother playing hockey. At age twelve, Michelle, eager to get to the nationals and the Olympics, secretly took and passed her senior test, even though her coach had advised her to stay in the junior level for another year. Later that year, after winning the Pacific Coast sectionals, Michelle competed at nationals, placing sixth. In 1993, Kwan qualified for the Olympic team as an alternate.

While she never won Olympic gold, she earned silver and bronze medals at the 1998 Nagano and 2002 Salt Lake City games, respectively. She competed at such a high level otherwise—five-time world champion and nine-time U.S. champion—that she's considered among the best figure skaters of all time and one of America's most beloved athletes.

A DAY IN THE LIFE OF A YOUNG PRO FIGURE SKATER

Taylor Webster began skating when she was eight, after she attended a friend's skating birthday party. After just a few years, she and her parents moved from their Florida home to live closer to a world-class training facility at the University of Delaware. By the age of twelve, she was training at the intermediate level and dreaming of going to the Olympics.

Taylor's day begins at 5:00 AM. After stretching and warming up, she is on the ice by 6:40 AM for the first of six on-ice sessions each day. At 8:30 AM, she leaves for school and returns to the rink at 3:00 PM for off-ice conditioning (including weight training and dance classes) before skating three more sessions. She finishes skating at 8:00 PM, then goes home for dinner and to do homework.

Taylor exhibits natural grace as she bends into a beautifully positioned and perfectly centered layback spin and smiles often when she talks about skating. She's realistic about her dreams and says, "I want to get through all my tests, even if I don't compete. My long-term goal is to get to the Olympics, but my goal this year is to get to the junior nationals and do the best I can there." Ultimately, Taylor Webster's reason for skating is, "Not so much to be a professional or to be famous, but because I love it."

Ashley Wagner

Another rising talent in American figure skating is Ashley Wagner. With a steady ascent up until the 2010 U.S. Nationals, in which she just missed placing on the U.S. Olympic Team, Wagner became infamous as "The Almost Girl." Spinal problems nearly put her career on hold over the next two years, but she moved to California, got a new coach and choreographer, and bounced back with a U.S. championship gold medal in 2012, and then again in 2013, being the only American to win back-to-back since Michelle Kwan in 2004 and 2005.

At the 2015 U.S. championships in Greensboro, North Carolina, Ashley Wagner won the ladies free skate program. American fans consider Wagner one of the hopes of modern skating.

Wagner placed a disappointing seventh in the 2014 Olympics after barely making the team to begin with. She bounced back yet again, however, when she set a new national record for points in her third U.S. title win in 2015.

Gracie Gold

Gracie Gold began skating at age eight while living in Springfield, Illinois, when she attended a friend's birthday party at an ice rink. After placing fourth on the novice level at the 2010 U.S.

Championships, her first major title was winning the ladies' gold medal at the ISU Junior Grand Prix in Estonia in 2011. Gold was the 2012 World Junior silver medalist, won the U.S. national silver medal in both 2013 and 2015, and placed fourth in the Sochi 2014 Winter Olympics in Russia overall, winning a bronze with the U.S. team. Many fans of the sport have high hopes that Gold will reach greater heights and put the United States back on the skating map at the medalist level.

Elizaveta Tuktamysheva

As with many winter sports, Russia has been a powerhouse in women's figure skating for years. As of September 2015, the top three skaters in the world, according to Icenetwork.com, were Russians. Elizaveta Tuktamisheva was at the top of the list, at age eighteen. Coming from a modest background, her family could not afford to move to a big city to give the promising young skater better training and coaching. She often made a twenty-seven-hour journey from her small hometown of Glasov to the skating mecca of St. Petersburg, Russia, to fully develop her talents there seven to ten days every month. This was in addition to her regular, daily training at home.

A skating wunderkind, she achieved the highest technical store during the free skate at the Russian national championships in 2008 at age eleven. Since then, she has won many titles, becoming the Russian champion (in 2013), European champion (2015), and the 2015 world champion as well.

Russia's Adelina Sotnikova competes in the ladies free skate contest in her homeland during the Sochi 2014 Winter Olympics, where she claimed the gold medal in ladies' singles.

Mao Asada

One need not be in the top three at any given time to be considered one of the greatest skaters. Ranked number eight in the world as of September 2015, Japanese skater Mao Asada consistently appears with her peers' on lists of the most admired figure skaters in the world.

A skating prodigy from early on, Asada has achieved fame for her grace, expressiveness of form, and for landing difficult moves. She was the silver medalist at the 2010 Olympics, her performance there notable because she landed three triple axels in a single competition, a feat unmatched by anyone else, and the first junior skater to land the triple axel (in the 2004–2005 Junior Grand Prix). Asada also holds the world record for the highest score achieved in the ladies' short program.

In an era where technical achievement has arguably become more important than the intangible, artistic aspects of figure skating, Mao Asada has been praised by observers of the sport and fans for skating artistic programs while being aggressively technical, too.

A GREAT JOURNEY

If you are ready to skate, there is no better time to get started. Remember that nothing is stopping you from getting as good and reaching as high as your natural talent and dedication can help you achieve. But make sure your goals are realistic, and that you put into skating only as much you realistically will get out of it.

You will find out early on whether you have the goods to get to the top. Most young girls and teens do not, and that is okay. The vast majority of high-level competitive skaters begin training at quite a young age (from four to six years of age). But someone starting out at twelve, thirteen, or even fifteen years of age can go far, even if they do not compete at a national level. Howeber, there is simply too much training necessary to start late and expect to excel by the time your stamina begins to slow down as you hit your late twenties.

Skating can still be a thrilling, productive, and life-changing experience. Doing it simply for the money or to win is not enough. Love of the sport and the activity itself is the most important thing. There are few things as relaxing and thrilling at the same time as gliding on the ice and putting hours of practice and sacrifice into a few minutes of superb performance. Remember that, and good luck on the ice!

1742 The first figure skating club is formed in Edinburgh, Scotland.

1882 Vienna, Austria, is the site of the first international skating competition.

1896 The first figure skating world championships are held in St. Petersburg, Russia. Open only to men, the contest resulted in a win for champion Albert Fuchs.

1902 Madge Syers is the first woman to compete in championship skating when she enters the men's competition. She surprises everyone by taking second place. Threatened by this success, the organizers ban women from men's competition.

1906 Separate world championships are held for women. Madge Syers is crowned the champion, a performance she would repeat the following year.

1908 Skating makes its first appearance in the Olympics.

1924 After much effort to create a separate Olympic event for winter sports, the first winter Olympics are held in Chamonix, France. Figure skating is the only women's sport during the competition.

1936 Sonja Henie wins her third Olympic gold medal for female singles in Bavaria, Germany (she won the other two in 1928 and 1932), one of many championships the famous skater would claim.

Cecelia Colledge of Great Britain performs the first double jump by a woman (a double Salchow) at the European Championships that year.

1947 Mollie Phillips becomes the first woman to judge an international figure skating event.

1956 Tenley Albright is the first American woman to win an Olympic gold in women's figure skating, in Cortina d'Ampezzo, Italy.

1961 Jana Mrazkova of Czechoslovakia and Helli Sengstschmid of Austria are reportedly the first women to perform a triple jump (triple Salchow) in competition.

1976 American Dorothy Hamill wins both the world championships and the Olympic gold medal at Innsbruck, Austria, and becomes one of the first big media stars of figure skating's modern era.

1983 Katarina Witt of East Germany, who later won Olympic gold twice in 1984 and 1988, won the first of her six consecutive European championships, a feat only beaten by Sonja Henie decades earlier.

1986 Debi Thomas is the first African-American woman to win the world championship in figure skating.

1988 Midori Ito of Japan is the first woman to land a triple jump combination (a triple toe–triple toe) at the 1988 NHK Trophy competition in Tokyo, Japan. She also does the first triple axel by a woman the following year.

1990 Skating "figures" is eliminated from professional competition.

1994 The Nancy Kerrigan/Tonya Harding rivalry and tabloid drama surrounding their Olympic face-off at Lillehammer, Norway, ends with Kerrigan earning a silver, losing to Ukraine's Oksana Baiul. It does have an explosive effect on ice skating's massive popularity during the remainder of the 1990s.

1998 Tara Lipinski, a fifteen-year-old from the United States, becomes the youngest woman to win an individual Olympic gold medal in figure skating at the games in Nagano, Japan.

2002 The Salt Lake City winter games is rocked by scandal, in which judges are accused of colluding to favor the victory of the Russian pairs figure skaters over their competitors. The scandal prompts the skating body in charge of international competition, the International Skating Union (ISU), to revamp the rules of competition.

2004 Newly revamped judging rules are rolled out for figure skating, favoring technical requirements, and these have remained controversial.

GLOSSARY

AXEL JUMP This jump starts from a forward skate, has an extra half rotation, and is landed with the skater gliding backwards.

EDGE Each skate has an inside and an outside edge with a hollow in the middle. A skater can skate on an inside or an outside edge, going either forward or backward.

EDGE JUMP A jump that takes off from an edge without using the other foot to assist. The axel, Salchow, and loop are edge jumps.

FLIP JUMP A toe jump that takes off from the back inside edge, assisted by the toe pick, and lands on the back outside edge of the opposite foot.

FREE LEG The leg that is not on the ice.

FREE SKATE The second and longer of the two programs that that make up a figure skating competition.

ROTATION The direction of a turn, jump, or spin. This can be clockwise or counterclockwise. Most skaters have a decided preference for one direction over the other.

SALCHOW JUMP An edge jump that takes off from the back inside edge, named after Ulrich Salchow.

SHORT PROGRAM The first and shorter of the two programs required by skaters in competiton, with certain required elements that must be completed.

SPIRAL An arabesque move in which the skater extends her free foot in the air behind her. A spiral can be executed moving forward or backward, on an inside edge or an outside edge, in a straight line or on a curve. The move shows flexibility.

STROKING A movement in which the skater pushes off from the inside edge of each skating foot alternately to gain speed.

THREE-TURN A turn, done on one skate, that involves changing both edge and direction. For example, a forward right three-turn begins on the right inside edge, going forward, and finishes on the right outside edge, going backward. The tracing on the ice looks like the number three.

TOE JUMP A jump that takes off assisted by a toe pick.

TOE LOOP A toe jump that takes off from a back outside edge, assisted by pushing up and off the opposite toe pick, and lands on the same back outside edge.

TOE PICK The teeth on the front of a figure skating blade.

WALTZ JUMP A basic half jump, and a foundation of the axel jump, which begins going forward on a left outside edge and lands on the right outside edge of the opposite foot.

WUNDERKIND A person who is very successful at something at a very young age.

FOR MORE INFORMATION

Ice Skating Institute
17120 North Dallas Parkway, Suite 140
Dallas, TX 75248
e-mail: isi@skateisi.org
Website: http://www.skateisi.com
The Ice Skating Institute is a trade association for those who
own and manage ice skating rinks, and also an international
governing body for recreational figure skating.

International Skating Union (ISU)
Chemin de Primerose 2
1007
Lausanne, Switzerland
+41 21-612-66-66
e-mail: info@isu.ch
Website: http://www.isu.org
The International Skating Union (ISU) is the international sport
federation administering ice skating events worldwide.

Professional Skaters Association (PSA)
3006 Allegro Park Southwest
Rochester, MN 55902
(507) 281-5122
e-mail: office@skatepsa.com
Website: http://www.skatepsa.com
The PSA is the official figure skating education, training and

accreditation program for coaches working with U.S. figure skating and the Ice Skating Institute.

Skate Canada
1600 James Naismith Drive, Suite 403
Gloucester, ON K1B 1C1
Canada
(613) 747-1007
e-mail: skatecanada@skatecanada.ca
Website: http://skatecanada.ca
Skate Canada works to promote skating sports, including figure skating, to Canadians, their schools, and communities.

United States Figure Skating Association (USFSA)
20 First Street
Colorado Springs, CO 80906
(719) 635-5200
Website: http://www.usfsa.org
U.S. Figure Skating (USFSA) is the national governing body for the sport of figure skating in the United States.

WEBSITES

Because of the changing number of Internet links, Rosen Publishing has developed an online list of websites related to the subject of this book. This site is updated regularly. Please use this link to access this list:

http://www.rosenlinks.com/IX/Skate

FOR FURTHER READING

Dzidrums, Christine. *Yuna Kim: Ice Queen* (Skate Stars). Los Angeles, CA: Creative Media Publishing, 2011.

Hile, Lori. *The Science of Snowboarding* (The Science of Speed). Mankato, MN: Capstone Press, 2014.

Hunter, Nick. *The Winter Olympics.* Chicago, IL: Heinemann-Raintree, 2014.

Koestler-Grack, Rachel A. *Michelle Kwan* (Asian Americans of Achievement). New York, NY: Chelsea House Publishers, 2007.

Mackay, Jennifer. *Figure Skating* (Science Behind Sports). San Diego, CA: Lucent Books, 2012.

Milton, Steve. *Figure Skating's Greatest Stars*. Richmond Hill, Ontario: Firefly Books, 2009.

Rendon, Leah. *Joannie Rochette: Canadian Ice Princess* (Skate Stars). Los Angeles, CA: Creative Media Publishing, 2010.

Shulman, Carole. *The Complete Book of Figure Skating*. Champaign, IL: Human Kinetics, 2001.

Strait, Raymond, and Leif Henie. *Sonja Henie: An Unsuspected Life*. New York, NY: Welcome Rain Publishers, 2015.

Thomas, Keltie, and Stephen MacEachern. *How Figure Skating Works* (How Sports Work). Toronto, Ontario: Owlkids Press, 2009.

Throp, Claire. *Figure Skating* (Winter Sports).Chicago, IL: Heinemann-Raintree, 2014.

Torvill, Jayne, and Christopher Dean. *Our Life on Ice: The Autobiography*. New York, NY: Simon & Schuster, 2015.

Ware, Susan. *Title IX: A Brief History with Documents*. Long Grove, IL: Waveland Press, 2014.

Yamaguchi, Kristi. *Figure Skating for Dummies*. Foster City, CA: International Data Group, 1997.

INDEX

W

ABOUT THE AUTHORS

Pete Michalski is an author from New York, New York. His books for young adults include titles on sports, including hunting, fishing, and winter sports.

Kathryn M. Moncrief is a professor and department chair in the English department at Washington College in Chestertown, Maryland. In addition to her published academic works, she is also a recreational skater and has written extensively online about figure skating.

CREDITS